TIME DOGS

BARRY AND THE GREAT MOUNTAIN RESCUE

TIME DOGS
BARRY AND THE GREAT
MOUNTAIN
RESCUE

Illustrated by

HELEN MOSS **MISA SABURI**

GODWINBOOKS

Henry Holt and Company 🐾 New York

Henry Holt and Company, *Publishers since 1866*
Henry Holt® is a registered trademark of Macmillan Publishing Group, LLC
120 Broadway, New York, NY 10271 • mackids.com

Library of Congress Control Number: 2019941047
ISBN 978-1-250-18637-9

Our books may be purchased in bulk for promotional, educational,
or business use. Please contact your local bookseller or the Macmillan
Corporate and Premium Sales Department at (800) 221-7945 ext. 5442
or by email at MacmillanSpecialMarkets@macmillan.com.

First edition, 2020 / Designed by April Ward and Sophie Erb
Printed in the United States of America by LSC Communications,
Harrisonburg, Virginia

1 3 5 7 9 10 8 6 4 2

TO STORM AND MAIA,
STILL PUPPIES AT HEART

1

IDEAS ARE TROUBLE

I was on the way to Perfect Pets when I had my bright idea.

I could barely keep still while the groomer was blow-drying my tail.

By the time my human lady, Ayesha, dropped me off at Happy Paws the next morning, I was fit to burst. I raced across the yard to the old cherry tree, where

Trevor, Baxter, and Newton were snoozing in the shade. One Jack Russell terrier, one yellow Labrador retriever, one black-and-white border collie. All snoring. "Wake up!" I panted.

Baxter snuffled. Trevor grunted.

Newton didn't stir. His hearing is not too good these days.

A revolting odor—*moldy salami, cat poop, pond slime*—wafted over from the long grass. It was Titch, of course. She was asleep on her back, all three legs pointing to the sky. Titch is *not* a genuine member of Happy Paws Farm, which is a high-class club for senior dogs. She just wanders in when she feels like it. Her personal hygiene is, quite frankly, criminal.

I tried again. "Wake up!" I shouted. "I've had an idea!"

"An *idea*?" said Titch, yawning. "Ideas are trouble, Puffball. I'd stick to prancing about and jumping over stuff if I were you."

My name is *not* Puffball, by the way. Titch just calls me that because she's jealous. We papillons have long, silky fur, and I keep mine in tip-top condition. Titch's fur is unkempt to say the least. My real name is Magical Mariposa, or Maia to my friends. "For your information," I pointed out, "you don't get to be All-State Champion three years straight by 'prancing about.' Dance routines take skill, focus—"

Titch yawned again, showing off her missing teeth.

I gave up. Titch would never understand Canine Freestyle dancing.

"*WAKE UP!*" I yelled at the others.

Trevor sprang up like a startled cat,

scattering a cloud of blossom petals. "Rat attack! Fight for your lives!"

"What's that?" spluttered Newton. "A bat attack?"

Baxter opened one eye and stretched. "*Rats*, Newt. Not bats." He grinned. "Invisible ones, I think."

"It's about the shiny box," I said, before they could fall asleep again. I glanced across at the van parked beside the barn. It *looked* like an ordinary van. It belongs to Baxter's girl, Lucy, and her grandma, who live at the farm. But it was far from ordinary. That van could zoom through the air like a giant bird. It had carried us off to faraway places. The silver box inside seemed to control it, but we had no idea how. *Until now*, that was. "I've figured out how it works."

Baxter's tail thumped the ground. "Is it magic?" he asked. "Like the garden hose. Water comes out. Who knows how? Then it stops. Starts. Stops. *Magic!* Or TV. Where do the noises come from? Or—"

"Stuffed crust pizza," Titch chipped in. "That's definitely magic. I mean, how do they make the cheese that *gooey*? Speaking of pizza, is it snack time yet?"

I was starting to wonder whether my friends even deserved to hear my idea—but it was just too good to keep to myself. "So, I was riding in the car yesterday when Ayesha took a wrong turn. She kept staring at the little screen on the dash. That's when it struck me. The screen had patterns on it—like the ones that flash on the shiny box when the van moves." I paused for effect. This was the best part. "I think humans use them to tell their vehicles where to go."

Baxter and Trevor were nodding, but their eyes had glazed over.

Luckily, Newton was keeping up. Border collies are always smart. "I think you may be onto something," he said. "Humans can't smell places like we do, so they use other ways to navigate."

I brushed away the blossoms and scratched two sets of lines in the dirt.

1925
1805

"The top pattern was flashing on the shiny box when the van took us to Alaska," I said. "And the bottom one was showing when we landed beside the Missouri River. You need a good memory for dance routines, too," I added, shooting a look at Titch.

Newton tipped his head to one side. "So, you think every place has its own special pattern?"

"Exactly," I said. "They're like scent markers for humans."

Trevor sniffed at the scratches in the dirt as if they might *actually* smell of Alaska and the Missouri River.

"That's crackers!" Titch laughed. "But hey, I'll take your word for it. Humans *are* crackers! They pick up poop in little bags, for goodness' sake!" She set off across the yard toward the van. "So, what are we waiting for?" she barked. "All aboard the freaky flying machine. Let's put Puffball's big idea to the test!"

2

THE SHINY BOX

The back doors of the van were open and we all jumped inside. It was fitted out like a cozy little house, with all kinds of furniture. Human tools and clothes were neatly stored on shelves and hooks. Bags and backpacks, a skateboard and a basketball were laid out on the bed. It looked as if Lucy and her grandma were planning a trip.

I hopped onto the driver's seat with

Newton. Baxter clambered onto the passenger seat, chewing on that soggy old tennis ball he always carries around. Trevor clambered up next to him—not easy for an elderly Jack Russell who hasn't kept himself in shape. Titch stood in back, craning her massive head through the gap.

We all gazed down at the shiny box between the seats. About the size of a shoebox (Ayesha *loves* shoes!), it was made of metal, with buttons, dials, and a dark glossy screen. Newton tapped his paw on the top. "I always suspected this was some kind of control panel," he said. "If Maia's theory is correct, we tell the van where we want to go by making it show the right pattern."

I pressed my nose to the box. It was as cold and still as a stone. "How do we start it up?"

"Watch and learn!" Titch leaned down and tried to head-butt the shiny box. She missed. Instead she knocked a can of soda flying out of the cup holder on the dash. Orange soda sprayed over everything— including me, my new pink ribbons, *and* my best cashmere coat. "Yum!" slurped Titch, licking my ears. "Delicious."

"Eugh!" I groaned, dodging away from her. If there's one thing worse than soda in your fur, it's Titch's stinky slobber all over it.

But somehow the shiny box had come to life. Bright lines and circles flickered across the surface like the sun sparkling on water: *0001, 0002, 0003.*

"Now let's see," murmured Newton. "How do we get the pattern for Alaska . . ."

Baxter wagged his tail. "Ooh yes. I'd like to see Balto and the other sled dogs."

"Who said we're going to Alaska?" barked Trevor. "As pack leader, I say we head back to the Missouri River. Catch up with our friend Seaman. Fight grizzly bears and go hunting again."

"Missouri gets my vote, too," said Titch. "All-you-can-eat buffalo meat. What's not to love?"

I wasn't so sure. I know it was my genius idea that had gotten us here, but I hadn't planned to zoom off on another adventure quite so soon. I'd vowed never to go *anywhere* in the van again without my travel bag. I wanted my special food, my herbal shampoo, my vitamin pills . . . "Wait! Let's take a rain check."

Too late! The doors slammed shut and the van rocketed into the air. *Ka-boom!* A whiff of thunder and firecrackers replaced the candy-sweet scent of soda. I rested my paws on the dashboard and looked out the windshield. We were already above the trees. The rooster weather vane on the barn spun around and around. A flock of chickens, scratching for worms in the yard, ran for cover, squawking and flapping. I knew how they felt.

Now the van was spinning, too. The others toppled over, but I kept my balance. I peered at the pattern on the shiny box. *1809 . . . 1808 . . . 1807.* It was *almost* the same as the pattern for the Missouri River. "Newton," I panted. "What do we do?"

But Newton was no help. "Bit dizzy," he mumbled. "Bumped my head on the steering wheel. Where am I?"

That, I thought, *is a very good question.* Outside, a whirlpool of shooting stars swirled through the dark. *No help there, either!* I looked back at the box. *1805.* That was the pattern for the Missouri River. How could I stop it from changing again? I turned to the others. Baxter was hiding behind his paws.

Trevor had gotten stuck under the passenger seat, yelping, *"All-Pack Alert! Don't panic!"*

The only one *not* freaking out was Titch.

I poked a paw at the box. Nothing happened.

Titch bellowed in my ear. "Do it like you *mean* it!"

I slammed both front paws down so hard I flipped right over and landed on top of Baxter.

It was not my smoothest move, but it did the trick.

The lines and circles stopped flickering.

3

LEVEL ONE PACK EMERGENCY

1800.

It was the wrong pattern.

I'd been too slow. I'd blown it. "You blockhead!" I fumed at myself. "You *catbrain!*"

"Don't beat yourself up, Puffball," said Titch. "We'll probably just land a mile or two upriver."

We didn't have to wait long to find out.

The jolting and spinning stopped. For one long, jittery moment—like waiting in the holding area for your turn to run out into the show ring—the van hung in midair.

Then, with a whoosh, we plummeted, down, down, down until we hit the ground.

I leaped over the seats and made for the back doors. I was the only one who could open them. "Hurry up!" barked Titch. "There's a buffalo steak with my name on it out there." With the others crowding behind me, I flipped up on my hind legs and pressed down the handles. Both doors flew open. A gust of wind almost tore them from their hinges. Another gust sent my ears flapping about my head. An endless vista of snowy mountain peaks stretched in all directions. Above us, the sky was a

bright, brittle blue. Below, a sea of white fog hid the rest of the world from view.

"Phooey!" grumbled Titch. "Snow! The shiny box has double-crossed us. We must have ended up in Alaska after all. The food was terrible here last time. Nothing but dried fish!"

Suddenly the van began to rock. My stomach rose and sank and rose and sank again. "Titch! Move!" I cried. "You're too heavy."

"No need to get personal," she muttered.

"Maia's right!" said Newton, quickly pushing Titch away from the doors. "It seems we've landed rather *precariously* on a narrow ridge. With all the weight at one end, we could tip over the edge at any moment . . ."

The van lurched the other way. Tools fell from the shelves. The basketball and skateboard slid off the bed and bounced and rolled about.

"This is a Level One Pack Emergency!" shouted Trevor. "Everyone, freeze!" Newton and Baxter hunkered down in the middle of the van. Even Titch followed orders for once and joined them. Trevor inched his way to my side and poked his nose out. "It's not Alaska," he said. "You could smell the sea on the breeze there." He sniffed deeply. "I'm getting pine trees . . . wood smoke . . . goats . . ."

I could smell those scents, too. But they were very faint, wafting up from far below. The frosty air nipped at my nostrils; not just cold, but kind of thin and fizzy, too.

That's when I realized: that was not ordinary fog down there. We were so high up we were looking down onto cloud.

"Let's go home," said Titch. "If there's no buffalo meat on the menu, I'd rather go check out the trash cans behind that new pizza place in town." She lumbered to her paws. The van swayed. Titch toppled sideways, crashing into Baxter, who fell onto the skateboard, which began to roll across the floor of the van . . .

"Watch out!" cried Newton. But it all happened so fast. For the briefest of moments, they were blocked by the table, but the table gave way, and the van tipped more, and they kept on rolling, picking up speed . . .

Then the skateboard—with Baxter on top—rolled right out through the doors.

4

ALL MY FAULT

Silhouetted against bright sky and white snow, the unlikely combination of a Labrador on a skateboard soared in a high arc, landed, and hurtled down the steep slope. They skidded wildly from side to side, faster and faster, until with a *crash!* they smashed into a jagged rock. The skateboard popped up. *Crack!* It smacked back down. The sound echoed around the mountain peaks.

I closed my eyes, bracing for the dreadful crunch as Baxter hit the rock, too.

But the crunch didn't come.

"He's landed in a snowdrift!" gasped Newton. I opened my eyes to see a puff of snow powder fly into the air. Baxter emerged, shaking snow from his fur.

"Careful!" I barked. "Keep still!" But it was too late. Baxter had slipped over. He began to slide farther down the mountainside. He came to a stop, at last, on a narrow ledge some way below the drift.

Then . . . nothing. I held my breath. There was no movement. Surely Baxter couldn't be . . . "Look what you did!" I snapped at Titch. "You're so clumsy."

Titch bared her teeth at me.

"Oh, no!" she said. "This is on you, Princess Fluffybutt. If it wasn't for you showing off with your fancy *theories* about patterns and places, we wouldn't be up here wobbling around on a pointy bit of mountain in the first place."

My stomach heaved. This time it wasn't the swaying of the van. Titch was right. This *was* all my fault. I *had* been showing off. It was like that time when we were on the banks of the Missouri with Seaman. I'd been showing off my dance skills and gotten myself dognapped. My friends had to rescue me then. And now I'd put them in danger again.

"He's alive!" barked Trevor.

Far below us, Baxter was standing up, looking around in confusion. A wave of relief washed over me.

"Don't worry!" Trevor shouted down to him. "We'll have you back in a jiffy!"

But Newton's ears were clamped down flat with worry. "We're at the top of a wall of ice and rock. It'll be impossible to climb back up."

Impossible or not, I had to help Baxter. I arched my tail, straightened my back, and held my head high.

If I was going to do this, I would do it in style.

5

EYES ON THE PRIZE

I jumped. Deep, powdery snow softened my landing.

On the downside, it almost buried me alive.

I burrowed out and picked my way down to Baxter on the narrow ledge below. We papillons are the mountain goats of the canine world—nimble and sure-footed. I was soon leaping from the last rock to land neatly by his side.

Somehow Baxter had kept hold of his tennis ball. He dropped it in order to greet me with a joyful shower of slobbery licks. I was so happy that he was okay that I didn't mind—even though he was sticking bits of yellow fluff all over the gummy patches of soda on my fur.

In fact, Baxter was *more* than okay. He was bouncing with energy.

He had also shrunk . . .

Of course! It always happened when we traveled in the van. We became pups again. Not tiny babies, but half-grown youngsters. No wonder landing in the snow had been easier than I expected. My legs were full of zip. The old ache in my hips had gone.

"I always wanted to try skateboarding," laughed Baxter. "No wonder Lucy likes it so much. It's a blast."

Thwumpf!

Thwumpf!

The sounds came from Newton and Trevor landing in the soft snow above us. I should have known they'd jump out of the van to help Baxter, too. Trevor is crazy about teamwork. For Newton, it's a border collie thing. He has the sheepdog's instinct to keep everyone together.

Titch, of course, had stayed behind. She's not what you'd call a team player.

"Last one back to the van is a cat's bottom," barked Trevor as he darted off up the mountain. He was strong and light on his paws, now that he was young again, too.

"No need to shout!" laughed Newton, racing after him. It seemed his hearing was back, as good as new.

We scrambled up the first stretch

without much difficulty. But then we came to the final slope. If you could call it a slope! It was an almost vertical tower of icy rock.

Baxter's ears and tail sagged. "That's basically a *wall*," he whimpered.

Impossible. That's what Newton had called it. For an ordinary dog, perhaps! But I was Magical Mariposa. I'd scampered up hundreds of A-frame obstacles in agility competitions. I'd soon make it to the top and find a way to help the others, too. I took a run up and jumped. Legs pumping, paws scrabbling, claws clinging to the ice . . .

I slid back down.

"*Cha-a-a-r-ge!*" cried Trevor, launching himself at the wall. He bounced right off it.

Newton paced up and down. "If I could just calculate the best angle . . ."

I glared at the stupid great lump of rock.

It was not going to beat me. *Focus!* I told myself. *Eyes on the prize!* I tried over and over. At last Trevor pulled me away. "Maia, stop!" he said. "You'll injure yourself."

I flopped down on the snow. *Defeated!* Every mistake I'd ever made paraded through my mind. The time I went over the double jump the wrong way in the agility final. The time I tripped over my ribbons in the talent show. The time—my ears burned with the shame of it—when I forgot to make a bathroom visit before the show started, and piddled next to the judges' table.

Back home, Ayesha kept all my trophies and rosettes in a big glass cabinet. I didn't deserve any of them. We would freeze on the mountainside. We would never see our humans again. It was all my fault.

I looked up at the van teetering at the top of the wall of rock. So near and yet so far! A gigantic bird had perched on the hood, its shaggy brown feathers puffed up against the cold. *A golden eagle!*

I shuddered. Its small dark eyes were watching our every move.

6

THE ONLY WAY IS DOWN

A sudden squall of wind whistled through the mountains. With a bone-quaking scrunch of metal on rock, the van began to spin on the ridge like a weather vane in a hurricane. The eagle soared away, long flight feathers spread like giant human hands.

"I'm not staying in this thing!" yelled Titch. "It's about to take off!" She hurled herself out of the van and crash-landed headfirst in the deep snow. We ran to dig her out. Even as a pup she looked as if she'd just been in a fight, with her missing leg, missing teeth, and bites out of her ears. But she still towered over the rest of us. "So, what's the plan, gang?" she asked casually, as if we had just met in the park.

"We can't get back to the van," wailed Baxter.

"But we c-c-can't stay here." My words rattled out through chattering teeth. "We'll f-f-freeze."

Titch scratched at a fleabite. "It's a no-brainer, then. We'll head *down*. There's bound to be a diner at the bottom. With a bit of luck, they'll leave some pizza lying around."

"Titch is correct," said Newton. "*Down* is our only option."

"Through *that?*" Baxter stared down at the layer of cloud.

"A bit of fog won't hurt you, buddy!" said Titch. "I've seen a lot worse than this. I spent a winter in San Francisco on the run from a gang of bulldogs . . ."

Titch continued her tall tale as we made our way down the mountain in single file. The cloud soon swallowed us whole—a mean, wet mist that slid its tentacles under our fur and hid everything but our own front paws and the tail of the dog in front. Soon even Titch fell silent. On we marched, with only the thudding of our hearts and the rasping of our breath for company.

Then we heard the barking.

The muffled calls wove and warbled through the cloud.

"It's a ghost," wailed Baxter, gnawing frantically on his tennis ball.

We could hear the words now. *"I'm over here! This way!"*

That was no ghost. It was a dog.

My ears were frosted with ice crystals, the feathery fur hanging in soggy tassels. But I did my best to angle them toward the voice. It belonged to a young male. He was trying to sound strong and brave, but not exactly succeeding.

"I'm still here. On the high path!"

"Sounds like he's lost," said Trevor. "What's he doing all the way up here?"

Titch shrugged. "Let's see. Maybe he crash-landed his flying van and accidentally skateboarded out of it. No, my mistake," she said. "That could never happen!"

7

THE BARKING BEACON

I'm over here!" The barking went on and on. *"Do not fear to approach me, for I am a friendly dog!"*

Baxter frowned. "Why doesn't he just shout *'Help!'?"*

"It's probably hypothermia," said Newton. "When you get very cold, your mind can start playing tricks on you."

"Come on," said Trevor, heading toward

the calls. "Never Leave a Dog Behind. It's not our pack motto for nothing, you know."

Titch groaned. "But the Invisible Barker is not even *in* our pack. Nor am I, for that matter. I'm a free spirit. A dog of the open road." She began stomping down a narrow path that wound through the snow and rocks. "Don't blame me if there's no pizza left when you get to the diner— *oomph—agggh!*" Titch stumbled and rolled down a steep bank. Newton raced down, grabbed her stump of a tail, and dragged her back. "All right, all right!" she grumbled. "Watch where you're putting your teeth."

We followed the barking until a dog-shaped figure loomed through the fog.

"You're safe now," Trevor called out. "We've found you!"

The young dog—a big brown-and-white mastiff with shaggy fur and floppy ears—almost jumped out of his skin. "What do you mean *you* found *me*?" he said. His voice was wobbly—not to mention croaky from nonstop barking. "I've found *you*!"

Newton thought for a moment. "Hmm . . . I'm not sure it's technically possible to find anything by sitting in one place, shouting."

"Of course it is!" said the mastiff. "That's the whole point. I'm a Barking Beacon."

Perhaps Newton was right about hypothermia. This guy was out to lunch!

"O-*kaay*," said Titch slowly. "I know I'm going to regret this, but what exactly is a Barking Beacon?"

The young dog puffed out his chest. "The official Great Saint Bernard's rescue drill is a three-dog operation," he recited. "One stays with the injured human. That's the Gentle Guardian. One fetches help. That's the Rapid Runner. And one is the Barking Beacon. That's me. My name's Barry, by the way. The Beacon keeps up a cheerful and reassuring barking signal to attract any other lost and weary travelers, who can then be taken to a safe refuge." He paused for breath. "So, *are* you guys lost and weary travelers?"

"Yes," said Baxter and Titch.

"No," said Trevor and Newton.

"Sort of," I said. "The shiny box brought us here, but we can't get back to our van."

Barry looked baffled. "Sorry, I have no idea what you just said." He sat up straight and began to recite again. "You are now located in the Swiss Alps, above the Great Saint Bernard Pass."

"Thanks for the geography lesson, Barky Boy," Titch cut in. "But how about you take us to this safe refuge of yours? I hope they've stocked up. This lost and weary traveler could eat a whole family-size stuffed-crust four seasons. With chili oil and extra anchovies."

Barry looked even more puzzled. "Um . . . well . . . I'm not sure that dogs count as travelers. I think it has to be humans. When Bella and Brio come back, I'll check."

"Bella and Brio?" I asked.

"The other members of the team," said Barry. "They're the experts. I'm still training. We were on patrol with Brother Francis, one of our humans, when we found a human lady stranded in the snow. Brio and Brother Francis stayed with her. Bella ran back down to fetch help. And I'm on Barking Beacon duty, in case there are more—"

"Lost and weary travelers," chanted Titch. "Yeah, we got that part."

At that moment a thin, high cry pierced the fog.

8

NO TURNING BACK

Our ears all pricked up.

The cry seemed to be coming from inside a bank of solid rock.

"That sounds like a human," whimpered Baxter, his tail drooping. "A frightened one."

Newton crept toward the rock, listening intently. "Male, I'd say. No more than a pup. And Baxter's right. He sounds terrified. I think he's trapped in there."

"Look over here!" called Trevor. "There's a crack . . ." He scrabbled at the gap as if digging out a rat. But even his tough terrier paws couldn't tunnel through rock.

Barry sniffed at the spot. "You'd have to be a baby marmot to get through there."

"Or," I said, "a very small dog." I pushed my head into the gap to demonstrate.

Before I knew it, Trevor had taken charge. "Excellent plan! We'll adopt Barry's rescue drill. Maia, you're the Gentle Guardian. You go in and look after the boy until help arrives. We need a Rapid Runner to fetch the humans. Barry, you're obviously the dog for the job. You know the way." He paused. "You *do* know where to find them, don't you?"

Barry's ears were trembling. At that moment I wasn't sure he could have found his own tail. "But I can't . . . Bella told me not to leave my post."

"Don't worry about that," said Trevor. "I'll clear it with her later."

"I'll come with you if you like," Baxter offered. "This cloud-fog gives me the creeps, too. But my friend Balto taught me that being scared is the biggest part of being brave." He dropped his tennis ball at Barry's paws. "Have a chew on this. It'll make you feel better."

"Good. Barry and Baxter, off you go," said Trevor. "Maia, are you ready?"

"Ready as I'll ever be," I muttered, squeezing into the crack in the rock. The sides crushed my shoulders and snagged my ears. Why did I say I could do this? I hate cramped spaces. I wriggled. I squirmed. I couldn't go on. But there was no turning back. *Literally!* Until a large paw shoved me from behind. "You're welcome!" shouted Titch.

I shot through the gap into a huge cave. Shafts of light sliced down through holes in the rock. Deep shadow filled the spaces in between. The air hung old and cold and still.

I spotted a movement. A small human lay huddled against the back wall.

"Hello!" I called, shivering inside my cashmerve coat.

"I'm here to help!" I know humans can't understand, but I did my best to sound—what did Barry call it?—*cheerful and reassuring.* I'm not sure it worked. My voice echoed around the cave in a spooky howl. The boy sat up. I took a step. Then I shrank back, my heart doing backflips. Very slowly, I slid my paw forward again. *Rock . . . rock . . . nothing!*

"What's happening?" Trevor shouted through the gap. "I need a mission update here."

"There's a crevasse!" I called back. "It splits the cave in two. The boy is on the other side."

One more step and I would have plunged over the edge.

THE QUEEN OF JUMPING OVER STUFF

Can you jump over it?" barked Trevor.

No way, I thought. The chasm in the floor of the cave yawned deep and black and wide.

A shaft of light picked out a thin ridge of rock that jutted out into the crevasse from the other side of it—as if pointing at me like a long human finger. If only it reached all the way across, it would form a bridge! But it was too short. There was still a big gap. I looked closely at the distance. Maybe I *could* jump that far. But the landing would be almost impossible. That finger of rock was *very* narrow. *You've done harder tricks before,* I told myself. *Remember that circus-style routine you did for the talent show final. A flying leap from the high platform onto a balance beam, a high-speed run to the end, and then a big jump onto a swing.* All wearing a frilly tutu. It had won me first prize. This would be just the same. Jump over the gap onto the ridge and run along it to the other side of the crevasse. And I was young again now. My bones and muscles were strong . . .

But it's over a bottomless pit this time! whined a small voice in my ear.

"If anyone can do it, you can, Puffball!"

Titch hollered through the gap. "You're the queen of jumping over stuff!"

Titch may drive me crazy, but I have to admit: she's an awesome cheerleader. I shook away the whiny voice in my ear. If Baxter and Barry could be brave, so could I. "Yes," I shouted. "I can do it."

I leaped.

I landed.

The ridge was so narrow there was barely room for my paws to fit side by side. It was slippery, too. One of my back paws slid off the rock, pedaling crazily in thin air. I swayed one way and then the other, fighting gravity with everything I had. At last, I had all four paws in place. That landing wasn't going to earn me any style points, but I'd made it. Before I could lose my balance again, I ran along the rocky spine. *Eyes front. Don't look down!*

At last I reached the other side of the chasm.

A stab of pain jolted through my left hind leg. I'd pulled a muscle. But there was no time to worry about that now. My nose was full of the distressing scents from the human child—*blood, loneliness, fear.* I ran to his side. He was ice-cold and shaking. He had injured his leg, too. Blood from a long gash stained his pants. "I'm Maia," I said, licking his nose in greeting. "I'm your Gentle Guardian."

The boy gave a great, shuddering sob and grabbed

me around the middle, squeezing me so tight I thought I'd burst. I yelped in alarm. Papillons are companion dogs. We love to be petted. But I wasn't used to human pups. I wasn't used to being crushed in a bear hug. Baxter would have been much better at this job. Lucy cuddles him all the time. Or Newton. His human family has a whole litter of youngsters. Even Trevor's human, Old Jim, has grandchildren who often visit and play with him.

But one thing I did know: I had to share what little warmth I had left in me. Blocking out the pain in my sore—and now very squashed—leg, I snuggled against the boy's chest.

Gradually, the boy relaxed. He began to stroke my fur. Sticky with soda, soggy with snow, and crusted with tennis-ball fluff, it must have felt like something a cat coughed up. But it seemed to help.

Little by little, he stopped crying.

Little by little, we both stopped shivering.

"Don't be scared, little dog," he murmured. "I'll look after you."

The only word I recognized was *dog*. But his voice was soft and kind. "Don't be scared, little human," I whispered back. "I'll look after you."

BOO-OO-OOMMMM!

The noise exploded through the cave.

It shook the roof and walls and rattled every tooth and claw in my body.

10

A DREAM OR A MEMORY

The noise stopped. A tense hush took its place. Rocks creaked. Drops dripped from icicles. The boy whimpered. I may have whimpered a little, too.

"Trevor?" I yelled. There was no reply. "Newton? Titch?"

Nothing.

At last I heard a frantic bark. "Maia! Situation report. Now!"

I never thought I'd be so happy to hear Trevor giving out orders. "What's happening?" I called back. "Are you guys okay?"

"Oh sure, we're peachy!" shouted Titch. "The van just came crashing down the mountain on a great wave of snow. Just about landed on top of us."

The light filtering through the cracks in the roof of the cave was fading fast. It would soon be dark. The boy had closed his eyes. I licked his ears to wake him. I was so tired I could hardly hold my head up.

He wouldn't make it through a long, cold night.

I wasn't sure I would, either.

"Puffball!" yelled Titch. "Talk to us!"

Newton's voice came next. "Maia, I'm worried you'll get hypothermia. Come out of the cave. The van is in reach now. We can shelter inside it."

Out of the cave meant jumping back over the crevasse. *Out of the cave* meant squeezing through the rock again. Could I do it? And even if I could, *out of the cave* meant leaving the boy behind.

I was *not* leaving the boy behind.

There had to be another way. "How did you get in here?" I barked, batting his chin with my paw in frustration. Perhaps the boy understood, because he opened his eyes and looked up. I followed his gaze to one of the holes in the cave roof. It was directly above us, and while most of the holes were little more than cracks, this one was big and round. *"Of course!"* I barked. "You *fell* through."

And if the hole was big enough to fall *in* through . . .

But the cold had its claws in me now. My thoughts swam in slow motion. *Then it's big enough to climb out* . . . I was sinking into sleep. *I just need to nap for a moment.* I shook myself awake. *The hole? Yes, it's big enough. But too high. We can't reach it.* My eyes were closing again. I was at a show with Ayesha.

After the dog events . . . an act with humans in big hats riding on horses . . . they're throwing ropes to catch the bulls that run around the ring.

I snapped my eyes open. Was that a dream or a memory?

It didn't matter.

It had sparked a flash of genius—even brighter than the one about patterns and places. That brainstorm had gotten us into this trouble. This one was going to get us out.

And I knew which of my friends would understand my plan.

"Newton!" I barked. "I have an idea."

11

DRASTIC ACTION

It was the longest wait of my life. Longer even than the split decision by the judges in my first Canine Freestyle final. I did my best to keep the boy awake by telling him the story of every competition I'd ever entered.

At last I heard voices above us. "Maia! Are you there?" I looked up at the big hole in the roof of the cave. Snow fell into my eyes. Then my heart leaped with joy. Two faces—one black and white, one white and tan—peered down at me.

"I'm here!" I yelled. "Do you have the rope?"

"Got it!" called Newton.

"Operation Rescue is a go!" shouted Trevor.

If I'd had the energy, I would have danced a victory jig. The first part of my plan was working. *Fetch a long rope from the van,* I'd told Newton. *Then search the top of the rocky bank for the hole that the boy fell through.* "Lower the rope through the hole!" I barked.

The end of the rope snaked into view. Closer and closer, until it was dangling above my nose. Now all I had to do was to attach it to the boy.

That's when I realized. I hadn't thought this part of the plan through.

The boy was barely conscious.

I nudged him in the ribs. He moaned. Then he drifted off again. I tried to push him into a sitting position. He flopped back down. "Wake up!" I bellowed in his ear. His eyelids fluttered.

I looked from the rope to the boy and from the boy to the rope. I had never bitten a human before. But this was an emergency. It called for drastic action.

"Sorry about this," I mumbled as I sank my teeth into his ankle. Not hard enough to draw blood, but hard enough to hurt. He shrieked. His leg kicked out. His eyes snapped open. I grabbed the rope in my teeth and thrust it toward him. He shrank back as if afraid that I would bite again. But then his face lit up. He'd seen the rope. He reached out and grasped at it.

"Pull!" I shouted to Trevor and Newton.

But the boy's grip was too weak. The rope slipped through his hands. It flew up, whipping against the cave wall.

Think, Maia, think! I yelled at myself. How did the humans catch the bulls in that show? The bulls didn't hold on to the ropes with their hooves! No. Now I remembered. The ropes looped over their heads . . . "Lower the rope again," I barked.

I tried *everything* to make a loop in that rope. I twisted it and twined it and pushed it and pulled it. All I got was a great big tangle with me tied up in the middle of it. I yelped in frustration. My cry seemed to jolt the boy to his senses. All of a sudden, he figured out what I was trying to do. Summoning up a last scrap of energy, he untangled the rope, wound it around his middle, and fumbled it into a knot.

"Pull!" I shouted up through the hole.

The rope went taut. But just as the boy began to rise up, he dropped back down. He was too heavy.

"Try again!" I heard Trevor bark. "Titch! Put your back into it!"

"Wait!" cried Newton. "Baxter and Barry are back. Grab onto this rope

with us, you two, and pull like crazy."

Slowly, jerkily, the rope hauled the boy up. But before he was far off the ground, he reached down and scooped me into his arms.

"I told you I'd look after you, little dog."

12

THE BIGGEST, SMALLEST HERO

We were out of the cave! Trevor, Newton, Titch, Baxter, and Barry all huddled close to keep us warm.

"The rescue party is on its way," said Barry. "The humans will be here any moment." He took up his Barking Beacon duty again, to guide them to the spot. *"We're over here! This way!"*

The boy refused to let go of me. I didn't

mind. I was weak with cold and my leg throbbed. I didn't mind that, either. We had saved the human! I didn't even mind Titch making fun of me. "I'm loving your new look!" she said, grinning at my bedraggled fur, tattered ribbons, and torn coat. "It's like you slept in a dumpster."

She didn't look too good herself. Even for Titch. Blood caked her mouth where the rope had cut in, and she could barely stand. She must have put her all into pulling the boy out of the cave. Not that she'd admit it. Titch didn't have much time for humans; *seriously overrated as a species*, was her usual comment.

The clouds had cleared, but it was almost dark now. A crescent moon was rising over the mountaintops. A black shadow circled overhead. "That'll be the rescue helicopter," said Titch. "About time!"

"*Hel-i-copter?*" asked Barry. "What's that?"

No one had the energy to explain. And it wasn't a helicopter anyway. It was the golden eagle. Somehow I was sure it was the one I'd seen before. It landed on a jagged pale gray rock—which promptly dissolved into thin air. I blinked. There was an odd shimmer, and the van appeared in its place. So *that's* where it had ended up when it was swept down the mountain on the snow wave!

I blinked again. A soft *pop!* and the rock was back. *Rock, van, rock, van;* it flickered from one to the other, like the images on Ayesha's TV. Finally, it settled back into being a rock. I wasn't as surprised as you might think. The van always camouflaged itself to blend in with the background.

The eagle didn't seem surprised, either. It flapped its wings but stayed on the rock.

Baxter, meanwhile, was digging something out of the snow nearby. "It's Lucy's skateboard," he shouted. "It must have been carried down on the snow wave, too."

He broke off at the sound of human voices. A string of lantern lights bobbed up the steep path. The men who carried them wore cloaks over long brown robes. They ran to the boy and lifted him—with me still clutched in his arms—onto a small wooden sled. They gave him a warm drink from a flask and wrapped him in a thick blanket, which almost suffocated me. I had to burrow my way out for air.

The other men were all hugging and

patting Barry. If humans had tails, they'd have been wagging like crazy. "You're a hero, Barry!" they cried. "You saved the child. And his little pet dog, too!"

Barry ran about in excited circles. "We pulled him out of the cave," he barked. "With a rope and everything! It was so cool . . ."

Suddenly he fell silent. An older female, with stiff back legs and white hairs around

her muzzle, had stormed onto the scene. She was followed by a male with black fur. The famous Bella and Brio, I guessed. "Who do you think you are, young pup?" demanded Bella. "I put you on Barking Beacon duty. You're not qualified to carry out high-risk rescue operations."

"Don't be too hard on him, Bella," said Brio. "Young Barry may not have stuck to the rules, but he's done a great job."

Trevor introduced himself. "Barry was acting under my orders," he said. "I'll fill you in with a full Pack Leader Report later."

Bella backed down. "Yes, well, the boy is safe. That's the most important thing."

"Baxter and Newton and Trevor and Titch were part of the rescue, too," Barry told her. "And Maia was the biggest hero of all." He galloped over to me and licked my nose. "The biggest, *smallest* hero! She squeezed into the cave and . . ."

My moment of glory was cut short by a loud thump. Titch had hit the deck.

"She's fainted," said Newton, sniffing her gently. "She's exhausted." He thought for a moment. "Baxter, bring the skateboard over here. Turn it upside down and help me roll Titch onto it."

One of the men tied a rope to the skateboard-sled. He peered at the wheels, shaking his head, as if he'd never seen a skateboard before. He looked pretty puzzled by Titch and the others, too. I'm sure he was wondering where we had all come from.

Bella, Brio, and Barry led the way down the mountain. Two of the humans pulled the sled I shared with the boy. Another pulled Titch. The other dogs trotted behind with the rest of the men. We hadn't gone far when Titch sat up. "Way to travel in style!" she laughed.

Then she barked at the man pulling her along. "Gee up, human! This lost and weary traveler has an urgent appointment with a stuffed-crust pizza."

13

THE OLD STORY

I awoke with a start. I was tucked in on a sofa with the rescued boy. The room was lit by candles and a fire crackled in a stone fireplace. A human lady in a long dress, with a blanket around her shoulders—his mother, I guessed—sat in a chair by the fire, watching over us.

The rise-and-fall sound of men singing drifted in from another part of the building.

I stretched. My left hind leg was swollen. I'd broken several claws too. But I was warm, comfortable, and—most important—alive. Alive and *very* hungry! I sniffed the air. *Wood smoke . . . candle wax.* But then: *meat, gravy, cheese . . .* I slipped out of the sleeping boy's arms and limped into the corridor, following my nose down a flight of stone steps to a huge kitchen.

The others were eating from a big wooden bowl.

"It's not pizza," slurped Titch, spattering gravy in all directions. "But it's not bad."

The bowl contained some kind of meat stew. Almost certainly not low-fat. Almost certainly not organic. My stomach growled. It didn't care. I pushed in between Newton and Baxter and joined the feast.

When we'd finished eating, Barry, Brio, and Bella took us to the barn that the dogs shared with the mules and goats. It wasn't quite what I'm used to (I have my own bathroom and a king-size basket at home), but it was warm and snug.

In a cozy corner, a mother lay in the hay with a litter of tiny puppies. "That's my sister, Bianca," said Brio proudly. He flopped down next to them. "I'm their favorite uncle!" he laughed, as the pups clambered over him, squealing in delight.

We all curled up and began to talk over the rescue. Now that Bella knew the full story, she had forgiven Barry for breaking the rules. "The human boy is called Luca," she explained. "He and his mother became separated from their pack. They were trying to cross the pass to Italy. The monks will look after them until they are strong enough to travel."

"Monks?" asked Newton.

"That's what humans here are called," said Barry. "Their job is to take care of other humans and worship their god."

I looked up from licking my injured leg and paw pads. *Worship?* So that's what the singing was about. I often went to church with Ayesha. They did a lot of singing there, too. Dogs have our own gods, of course. We don't sing to them. But, like the monks, it is our duty to look after humans. In fact, Bianca was telling the old story to her puppies right now. The story we'd all heard from our mothers.

"Long, long ago, when dogs roamed with the wild wolves, the Great Hound was walking in the forest when a poisoned thorn entered his paw. On hearing his howls of pain, a human boy pulled out the thorn and saved his life. To repay him, the Great Hound vowed that from that day on, all dogs would live with humans and help them . . ."

Make that most dogs, I thought. Not Titch. I couldn't really blame her. She'd met humans who treated her badly. She had the scars to prove it.

"You're welcome to stay here as long as you like," said Bella.

"Thank you," said Trevor. "We could use a few days to get our strength back. But then we have to get home to our own humans."

The mules brayed grumpily. A goat stamped its hoof. Our chatter was keeping them awake.

Not for long. One by one, we closed our eyes and fell asleep, Bianca's bedtime stories weaving through our dreams.

14

NOT PERFECT

Staying there at the Great Saint Bernard Hospice was like a mini spa holiday.

Spring sunshine sparkled on the white mountains and warmed the ancient stone walls of the hospice buildings. In the valleys below, the snow had already melted. The meadows were green and full of wildflowers.

Cows and goats grazed. The *clank-clank* of the bells they wore rang softly on the breeze.

Trevor enjoyed hunting rats in the cellars. Baxter and Barry took Bianca's puppies outside for their first playtime in the snow. Newton and Brio worked on a design for a backpack the dogs could carry, equipped with blankets and flasks of hot tea. Titch didn't get her stuffed-crust pizza, but she found the next best thing. The monks made their own cheese!

"Great big smelly wheels of the stuff," she whooped. "A whole cellar full!"

She appointed herself chief taster.

As for me, I was busy looking after Luca. He was soon sitting up. His skin grew pinker, his eyes brighter. One of the monks found him a hairbrush so that he could groom my fur. I can't tell you how good it felt to get those tangles out! His mother sewed me a little red coat from a blanket. "Goodgirl, Angel," they murmured as they worked.

They seemed to think that Angel was my name. It was better than Puffball or Princess Fluffybutt!

After a few days Luca was well enough to sit outside in the sunshine. While he was playing with the puppies, I practiced my new samba dance routine.

But my injured leg was still weak. Nothing was going right. *No, that's not it!* I snapped at myself. *Do that move again!*

I didn't notice that Barry had stopped by to watch. "What are you doing?" he asked.

I explained Canine Freestyle.

"Wow!" he breathed. "You're a hero *and* an awesome dancer!"

"No, I'm not. I suck," I grumbled. "I keep making mistakes."

Barry laughed. "So, you're not *perfect?* You don't have to be perfect to be awesome. I wish I could be half as not-perfect as you. I get *everything* wrong. That's why Bella only lets me be the Barking Beacon." He sighed. "I've got an Avalanche Search class this afternoon. No doubt I'll mess up. As always."

I knew by now that *avalanche* was the proper word for the snow waves that thundered down the mountains.

"Why don't I come along?" I offered. "Maybe I can help."

The Avalanche Search training drill was simple. Brother Francis and the other monks buried objects in the snow. The dogs took turns finding them and digging them up. I soon figured out Barry's problem. He was so eager to please he couldn't focus on the task.

"Stay calm," I told him. "Remember, humans can't communicate with their ears or tails. Follow their eyes. Look where they're looking."

On the next try Barry did much better.

The others gathered around, all giving their advice.

"Use your *nose*!" yapped Trevor.

"*Think* through the problem," said Newton.

"Don't be scared!" barked Baxter.

Even Titch cheered him on. "You've got this, Barky Boy!"

Barry was soon at the top of the class.

"You were awesome," I told him later, when we all went for our evening stroll. The last rays of sunshine cast long shadows across the snow. "Almost *perfect*, in fact."

Barry wagged his tail. "I wish you guys could stay forever."

I almost wished we could, too. But I was missing Ayesha.

I've lived with her ever since I left my mother's basket and Ayesha moved into her own apartment. We're only apart when she goes to work (and I go to Happy Paws). She needs me there.

The others were eager to get home to their human families, too—except Titch, who is a stray and so doesn't have one. "We'll leave tomorrow," said Trevor.

The first stars twinkled in the gathering dusk. I would miss the mountains. I would miss Barry and the other rescue dogs. I

would miss Luca. One thing I *wouldn't* miss, I thought, as a great golden-brown bird skimmed the skyline on whispering wings.

That eagle.

My hackles stood up.

It was *definitely* watching us.

15

GOODBYE, LITTLE DOG

We were not the only ones getting ready to leave.

Next morning, Luca and his mother were up at first light.

I watched sadly from the steps of the hospice as they met with the mountain guide who would take them over the pass. He was leading two mules. The guide helped Luca's mother onto one of them. Then he reached down to help Luca onto the other mule, but the boy pulled away. "I'm not going without Angel!" he cried, snatching me up in his arms.

I tried to wriggle free. I had grown to love Luca—even his bear hugs. But I already had a human to look after.

Trevor, Baxter, and Newton jumped up, barking. "Let Maia go! You can't take her!"

"Get your greedy little paws off her, human child!" growled Titch.

"I'm sorry," Brother Francis said to Luca's mother. "It looks like Angel's pack really don't want to part with her." Then he spoke softly to Luca, took me from his

arms, and set me down next to Trevor. Tears streamed down the boy's face. I felt like crying, too. I couldn't go with him, but I hated to leave him like this.

"Wait," said Brio. "I've got an idea." He ran to the barn. Moments later, he returned with Bianca and the puppies. He pushed forward the smallest of the litter, a little ball of brown-and-white fluff.

I looked at Bianca. Surely she wouldn't give up her puppy? But Bianca was nodding. "It's time for the pups to leave the basket," she said. "Bobby is too small to train for the rescue team. We were going to find a human family down in the valley for him. But I've seen how kind Luca has been to Maia. I'd be happy for him to take Bobby." Bobby wagged his tail so hard he fell over. "Can I really go with them, Mom? To Italy! On an adventure!"

Bianca gave him a big lick on the nose. "Yes, you can. Be good. Remember your manners. Do your duty." She picked Bobby up by his scruff and placed him gently on Luca's feet. Luca looked up at his mother. She smiled. He crouched down and buried his face in the puppy's soft fur.

The boy reached out a hand and stroked my ears one last time. I licked away his tears. Then he climbed onto the mule, carrying Bobby in a sling made from a blanket. As they set off, he looked back. "Goodbye, little dog," he called.

"Goodbye, little human," I barked. "Stay safe."

16

LAUGHING IN THE FACE OF DANGER

We were about to go inside for breakfast when we heard the noise. Bangs and clangs and human shouts floated up from the lower slopes on the frosty air.

Then came the smells. *Sweat, mud, brandy, gunpowder.*

A vast crowd of men soon began to appear, marching up the Great Saint Bernard Pass, beating drums, waving flags,

and firing guns into the air. All wore the same outfits: dusty blue jackets, white trousers, and black boots and hats. There were mules, too, piled high with equipment.

Trevor's hackles flicked up. "What the blazes is going on?"

"I don't care," whimpered Baxter, looking around for his tennis ball. "It's too loud. Make it stop."

"Hey, you!" yelled Titch, spotting a dog among the commotion. A large black poodle was strutting up and down, shouting orders. His fur was clipped into a peculiar style: short at the back, with a woolly mane at the front. I thought Titch's personal hygiene was bad, but this guy was in a different league. *Fleas, ticks, mites* . . . that mane was an entire ecosystem. He smelled even worse than the men did. They must have been on the road a long time. "Yeah, you with the goofy haircut!" Titch barked. "Is this some kind of carnival parade?"

The poodle stamped his paw. "How dare you address an officer like that! Where's your leader?"

"That's me," said Trevor, bowing politely. "Trevor's the name. But we're guests here. It's Bella you need to check in with. This is her territory. She's out on patrol with Brother Francis at the moment."

"Do you know who I am?" roared the poodle.

We clearly didn't, but he wasn't waiting for us. "I am General Moustache of the mighty French army. Second in command to Napoleon himself. And General Moustache does not 'check in.' General Moustache goes wherever he pleases." He broke off to holler at a pair of mules, who were dragging a huge gun. "Take it to the stores, you buffoons!"

"You're soldiers?" asked Newton. "Who are you fighting?"

"The bad guys, of course," said Moustache.

"But the monks aren't *bad*," said Baxter. "They rescue travelers and make cheese and do a lot of singing."

"Not *here*, you nincompoop!" barked Moustache. "We're crossing the pass into Italy. We'll take those scoundrels by surprise."

Titch laughed. "Good luck with that, buddy. They'll smell you coming a mile off."

Moustache ignored her. Narrowing his eyes, he stared up at the mountains. "I need to scope this place out before my men make camp for the night. There could be enemies hiding up there."

"You can't go on your own!" said Barry. "It's against the rules. It's dangerous."

"Pah!" snorted Moustache. "The mighty French army laughs in the face of danger." Then he paused. "Although a local guide or two is not a bad idea." He pointed at Barry. "I'll take you. And you," he told Titch. "You look like a soldier. Where did you lose that leg? Cannon fire, was it?"

Titch rolled her eyes. "New Jersey. Argument with a mail truck."

"'New Jersey'? Never heard of it. Must have been a minor battle. And what's a 'mail truck'? Some newfangled weapon, is it? I took a bullet to the shoulder in my last battle, you know." Moustache turned to Baxter and Newton. "You two look useful. You're a bit on the short side," he added, waving a paw at Trevor, "but you may as well come along. Quick march."

I cleared my throat. "What about me?"

Moustache laughed. "But you're just a silly little lapdog. Wouldn't want to get that pretty coat dirty, would we? Run along inside and find some fancy ladies to feed you sugarplums."

I was speechless with rage. Luckily, Titch was not. "Did I hear that right?"

She towered over Moustache and stuck out one ear—the one with the big bite out of it. "Did you just call my friend a *silly little lapdog*?"

"Maia's a *hero*," said Barry.

The others all agreed. "Come on, pack," barked Trevor. "We're out of here."

"Suit yourselves. You'd only slow me down anyway." With a flick of his pom-pom tail, Moustache headed off at a brisk march.

As we watched him go, I thanked my friends for sticking up for me.

"Don't mention it," said Titch. "You may be a puffball, but you're *our* puffball."

"*A bit on the short side*," fumed Trevor. "By jiminy! I hope we don't run into *him* again."

But Barry looked anxious. "There's a storm coming. He could get lost."

"Or fall into a crevasse," added Newton.

Baxter looked up from his tennis ball. "Or be eaten by wolves . . ."

Part of me thought that the wolves were welcome to him.

But snow was swirling. Storm clouds were gathering. In the distance, Moustache was a small black dot on a big white mountainside.

We had to go after him.

17

AMBUSH

When we caught up with Moustache, he was crouching behind a snowdrift halfway down a long, steep slope.

Barry called out to him. "Come back down before the blizzard sets in."

"Silence! Silence in the ranks!" growled Moustache. He was staring intently up at a crag of rock near the top of the slope. "I have an enemy position in my sights."

I peered through the snow, which was now falling thick and fast. I caught a flash of movement on the crag.

"It's w-w-wolves, isn't it?" whimpered Baxter. "I *knew* there'd be wolves."

Moustache didn't take his eyes off the "enemy position." "It's not wolves, you nincompoop! It's the bad guys. Three of them. Planning an ambush, no doubt."

Trevor squared up to him. "Barry's right. We need to get off the mountain. You have your information. Go report back to your humans."

Moustache fluffed himself out like an angry porcupine. "General Moustache does not 'report back.' General Moustache *takes action*." And with those words, he was away; charging toward the men's hideout. "Surrender, you scoundrels!" he barked.

"In the name of the mighty French *aghh!*" He slipped on an icy rock and rolled partway back down the slope.

A man's head popped up over the crag. He saw Moustache, aimed his gun, fired—and missed. The bullet whizzed into the snow, sending up a puff of spray.

Before he could shoot again, another man pulled the gun away. "It's just a dog!" he laughed. He hurried down the slope, carrying a canvas sack. Moustache barked and leaped up to attack, but then staggered and sank back down. He must have hit his head on a rock when he fell. The man bundled him into the sack, closed it with a drawstring, hoisted it over his shoulder, and carried it back up to the hideout.

Baxter dropped his tennis ball. "What do we do now?" he gulped.

"Go back for breakfast, of course," said Titch. "I'm planning one last cheese feast before we check out of this place."

"What about Moustache?" I said.

Titch shrugged. "He's a general. He can look after himself."

But Trevor shook his head. "Never Leave a Dog Behind, remember."

"I could free him from that sack," I said. "Ayesha taught me how to open a drawstring bag for a talent-show trick."

Titch laughed. "How does that work?

You just march up and say, 'Excuse me, humans, while I get my annoying poodle back'?"

She had a point. My "rescue plan" had slipped out of my mouth before I'd thought it through. I was going off the idea already. But now that I'd suggested it, I couldn't back out. "I'll sneak into their hideout," I said. "Humans have terrible eyesight. They won't see me through the snow."

It didn't sound very convincing, even to me.

But Trevor's tail was wagging. "The rest of us will make a big commotion— howl like wolves or something. The men will run out to see what's happening. Maia, you can go in while they're distracted."

Newton scratched his ear. "I don't like it. It's too dangerous for one dog alone." He looked out, scanning the area around the slope. "I'll go with Maia. If we circle around in a wide arc, we can drop into the hideout from behind. Classic sheepherding maneuver."

"Agreed!" said Trevor. "Everyone ready?"

Baxter and Barry looked terrified. The tennis ball had split in two, and they each had a piece clamped in their jaws. But they nodded. "Ready!" they said in unison.

"Well, good luck," said Titch, making to leave.

"Oh no you don't!" snapped Trevor. "We

need you for wolf-howl duty. You're the loudest of us all."

Titch groaned. "I don't believe this! We're actually putting our tails on the line for that puffed-up poodle?"

But she stayed.

18

SKY-WEAPON

*F*or once, I thought, as I crept up the slope, *I should have listened to Titch.* I was risking my life for someone who'd called me a silly little lapdog!

I stuck close to Newton, following his paw prints, trying not to sink into the snow. At last we were in position above the crag. We could hear the men talking . . .

Woo-hoo-hoo! A cacophony of wailing burst out from behind the snowdrift. My friends may have been aiming for the blood-curdling howls of a man-eating wolf pack, but it sounded more like a catfight. But it was certainly loud. And it worked. The three men ran out from their hideout, waving their guns.

"Go on, Maia!" said Newton. "I'll keep a lookout."

My heart was thumping as I approached the hideout. If the men turned back, they would spot me in an instant. It's true that humans don't see well in low light. And my markings are good camouflage against snow and rock. But I'd forgotten I was wearing my bright red blanket coat. I was not exactly dressed for a stealth mission.

But I made it. There was the sack, lying among the rocks. Muffled barks came from within. "I am General Moustache! I demand to be released! This instant!"

"Keep still, then!" I snapped as I pinned down the top of the sack with my paw. I tried to grab the other side of the opening in my teeth. Moustache was wriggling so much that it kept getting away. At last I got a grip on the canvas and tugged. The sack began to open. Moustache's muzzle poked out.

I pulled the sack open wider. Moustache's front legs were out now. He smelled worse than ever. His stinky mane was caked in grime and hopping with fleas. Then I caught sight of a big fat tick. I shrank back with a yelp of disgust.

Oh no! What was that? The crunch of heavy boots on snow. The men were returning.

"Maia! Run!" shouted Newton. "*NOW!*"

But it was too late. The boots were right behind me. "Get back in!" I hissed, pushing Moustache into the sack and ducking in after him. We would have to hide and wait it out.

The inside of the sack was gross: cramped, smelly, sticky, and crawling with bugs.

But I soon had more to worry about than getting fleas in my fur. All of a sudden the sack—with us inside—jerked up into the air. One of the men must have picked us up. But then I heard flapping, squawking, and human shrieks of fright.

We rose high into the sky, swinging from side to side. My stomach heaved. "What is this?" raged Moustache. "Some kind of newfangled *sky-weapon*? Put me down at once. Napoleon will hear of this! General Moustache is not a sparrow! He does not *fly*!"

But I knew *exactly* what was carrying us off.

It was not a sky-weapon.

But it did have a razor-sharp beak and killer talons.

19

LUCKY ESCAPE

I had never felt so miserable. If only I had worked faster. If only I hadn't been in a red coat. If only I hadn't yelped at Moustache's mangy mane. The men must have seen or heard me. That was why they came back so fast. The eagle had spotted me, too. Now it was carrying us off to feed to its chicks.

Moustache was still yelling. "Put me down at once, I command you!"

To my astonishment the eagle obeyed. We swooped in a long, swift dive. Suddenly we were on the ground, tumbling out of the sack into the snow. I heard familiar voices. *Baxter, Trevor, Titch, Barry . . .*

The eagle had set us down behind the snowdrift.

It had not been attacking. It had carried us to safety.

I looked up to say thank you, but it had already flown away.

Newton ran to join us. "Thank goodness you're safe, Maia," he panted. "I tried to warn you, but it was too late."

Trevor smiled. "Good work, both of you."

"Wow!" said Baxter. "That was so cool.

Maia! What an awesome idea to get the eagle to carry you out of the hideout."

"You're a *double* hero!" cheered Barry.

How could I explain? I was not a hero. I'd made a heap of mistakes. I'd just had a lucky escape. But then I remembered Barry's words. *You don't have to be perfect to be awesome.* I looked around at my friends, all exhausted and shivering with cold. Trevor was bossy. Newton was a worrier. Baxter was afraid of everything. Barry was nervous.

And Titch? Well, Titch was Titch. She was rolling around, pretending to gasp for

air because I smelled like that disgusting sack. "What is that new perfume you're using, Princess Fluffybutt?" she laughed. "Essence of poodle poop?"

Not one of them was perfect. But they were all awesome. They were all heroes.

Maybe I didn't need to be perfect, either.

Moustache nudged my shoulder. It made me jump. I'd almost forgotten he was there. "Not bad for a lapdog," he mumbled. "Although I had the situation under total control."

Titch snorted. "Obviously! You were just controlling it from *inside a sack*."

Moustache snarled at her. "General Moustache always waits for the right moment to spring out and take the enemy by surprise."

"Oh no!" gasped Barry.

Moustache turned on him. "Are you disagreeing with an officer?"

But Barry did not reply. His ears quivered.

"*Avalanche*," he breathed. "It's coming this way."

20

AVALANCHE

We could all sense it now.

The air pulsed. My ears tingled. Then came a deep cracking noise. A low *wumpf!* A rumble like distant thunder.

"Run for it!" yelled Barry.

We didn't wait to be told twice. We hurtled after Barry as fast as our legs would carry us, scrambling for a rocky outcrop off to one side of that long, steep slope.

"We're okay here," he panted, stopping in the shelter of a jagged pale gray rock. We turned to look back. A wall of snow was powering down the mountain like an army of runaway trucks.

"Oh no!" gasped Baxter. "The humans!" The three men who had been planning the ambush were still standing in the open near the top of the slope, directly in the path of the avalanche. They were pointing their guns up the mountain as if they could simply shoot the snow away.

"What *buffoons!*" snorted Moustache.

Baxter and Trevor wanted to dash back to help the men, but Barry and Newton stopped them. It was too late to reach the humans and drag them to safety. Instead we tried to warn them. "Run!" we shouted. "This way!"

Deafened by the rumble of the avalanche, the men didn't hear us. Frozen by fear, they didn't move.

We tried again. Even Titch joined in. "Move, you two-legged nitwits!"

At last the men looked our way. The sight of us seemed to jolt them out of their trance. They dropped their guns and raced toward us.

One of the men made it. The other two were caught in the snow.

"What's happening?" The voice belonged to Bella. We spun around to see her hurrying up behind us, followed by Brio and several of the monks. They had climbed the mountain by a different route and avoided the torrent of snow.

"We heard the avalanche and barking," called Brio. "We've come to help."

It didn't take long to dig the two men out. Fortunately, they had made it almost to the edge of the avalanche, so they had not been buried very deep. Barry led the entire operation. "Good work!" said Bella. "You've earned yourself a promotion to rescue leader for this. No more Barking Beacon for you!"

The monks wrapped the cold and shaken men in blankets for the journey down the mountain. "They'll be well taken care of now," said Brio.

"But these are enemy agents!" spluttered Moustache. "They must be handed over to the French army for punishment."

Barry squared up to him. He was no longer afraid of General Moustache. "There are no enemies at the Great Saint Bernard Hospice," he said. "We look after *all* lost and weary travelers, whoever they are."

"And talking of travelers," said Trevor, "it's time for us to leave."

It was hard to say goodbye. "You have all taught me so much," said Barry. "Especially you, Maia."

But the truth was, Barry had taught me more than I had taught him. "You're going to be a great rescue dog," I said. "A true hero of the mountains."

Barry picked up his half of the tennis ball and returned it to Baxter.

"Keep it," said Baxter. "It will help you to be brave."

"So long, Barky Boy," said Titch. "Save me some cheese for next time."

We didn't have to go far to find the van. Part of the jagged outcrop above us was no ordinary lump of pale gray rock. We all recognized its scent of metal and rubber and gasoline. Trevor pressed his nose against it. *Pop!* The van was back again. It was leaning at a precarious angle, and one of the back doors hung open.

We were about to climb in when the eagle landed on the roof.

Hunching its shoulders, it glared down at us. I shrank back. Had it changed its mind and decided to feed us to its chicks after all?

The eagle opened its hooked yellow beak. "Maia!" it squawked. "I need to talk to you."

21

AN IMPORTANT MISSION

Most dogs don't understand birds, of course. But I learned from Alphonse, the old African gray parrot who lives on our neighbor's balcony. He got bored of mimicking human cuss words years ago and decided to teach me bird language to pass the time.

But how did this eagle even know my name? I must have been staring with my mouth open, because it laughed. "Alphonse told me that you were smart for a dog. I'm not so sure."

"Sor-ry," I said, struggling to form the strange words. "This . . . just . . . surprise." Bird language is more a kind of squeaky singing than actual talking. "You are friend . . . of Alphonse?"

"Not in person," said the eagle. "But we exchange a lot of time-messages. My name is Kyra, by the way."

Titch head-butted my side. "Whoa, this is freaky!" she said. "Are you actually talking to a *bird*?"

I took no notice. "What is . . . *time-message*?" I asked Kyra.

Kyra hopped down from the roof. "I'll explain," she said. "But let's get inside this strange contraption first. You dogs look cold."

It was true. We were all shivering. "The eagle seems to be a friend," I whispered to Trevor as we climbed into the van. "She has something to tell us."

Kyra perched awkwardly on the bed. "All birds can send and receive messages across time," she said. "We talk about what has been and what will be. We make sure the winds of time blow free." She glanced around the van. Trevor and Newton were bursting to know what was going on. Baxter was chewing on the remaining scrap of his tennis ball, staring fearfully at Kyra's

talons. Titch was under the table, already snoring. "And so," the eagle went on, "when you guys started wandering through time, there was a *lot* of news going to and fro . . ."

"What's this all about?" barked Trevor.

I tried to explain. "Kyra says that we've been 'wandering through time' . . ."

Newton's ears flicked up. He ran to the shiny box. "*Of course! Time!* The patterns mean different years, not different places."

Kyra smoothed down a wing feather with her beak. "Time-messages were flying around. A pack of dogs kept popping up out of nowhere in a peculiar vehicle. Alaska, 1925. Missouri River, 1805. And now, Switzerland. 1800."

I was doing the openmouthed-staring thing again. *Birds had been spying on us?* Now that I thought about it, there *had* been a raven or a crow hanging around the van every time we'd taken off or landed. Although when we left Happy Paws Farm this time, there had only been . . .

"Chickens?" I asked. "*Spy chickens?*"

Kyra laughed. "They're not the best time-talkers, I'll admit. The message was a little garbled, but they got it through in the end." Then she fixed me with her sharp eyes. "This van can travel in time because it contains an object of great power."

"The shiny box?" I gasped.

"Not the box, but what is inside it. A golden collar. It belonged to a dog called Anubis, who lived in Egypt more than three thousand years ago."

My head was spinning. *How did an ancient magic collar end up at Happy Paws Farm?*

Kyra seemed to read my thoughts. "The golden collar was stolen by bad humans. It changed hands many times. Somehow it found its way to America, where it was buried in a field—until Baxter's humans found it. There is writing on the collar that tells of its powers. That's how Lucy and her grandmother—Professor Wells—learned that it could travel in time. They installed it in this van. But, unlike you dogs, they have not yet figured out how to *activate* the power."

We haven't exactly figured it out, either, I thought. The shiny box—or rather the collar inside—seemed to start up at random.

"You must return the golden collar to Anubis." Kyra shook her head sadly. "If humans figure out how to travel in time, it will mean disaster and destruction for all of us."

"But Baxter's humans . . . are good," I said.

"Maybe. But many others are not. And even good humans can be foolish. Their species cannot be trusted with so great a power."

"But why us?" I asked.

"Because dogs *always* look after humans," said Kyra. "You can save them from themselves." She shuffled toward the shiny box. "I will make it send you back to ancient Egypt."

"Wait," I shouted.

I explained Kyra's request to the others. Newton frowned, thinking so hard he went cross-eyed. There was a lot to think about! But Trevor simply turned to the eagle, his tail held high. "Yes. We will do our duty and accept this mission."

"But I want to go home," whimpered Baxter.

I felt the same way. "We'll do it," I told Kyra in bird language. "But first . . . we go see . . . our humans."

"I can give you a few days," she said. "No more. Professor Wells is dangerously close to learning how to activate the collar." She tapped the shiny box with her beak. "It will take you home now. Good luck!"

Kyra flew out of the van. The doors banged shut behind her. Titch woke up and yawned. "Has that pesky eagle buzzed off yet?"

We gathered around the shiny box. The pattern *2018* showed on the top, but nothing was happening. Titch pushed her head between the seats and shook melting snow all over us.

Beep, flash, rattle.

The van shot into the air.

We had an important mission.

But first we were going home. I couldn't wait to dance with Ayesha again. I'd need another visit to Perfect Pets, too. It was going to take some extra-strong shampoo to get the smell of that sack out of my fur.

AUTHOR'S NOTE

Although Trevor, Baxter, Maia, Newton, and Titch are fictional characters, many of the dogs they meet on their travels through time really existed. Their adventures together are inspired by actual events; events in which the real dogs played a crucial part.

The Great Saint Bernard Hospice is a real place. High in the Swiss Alps, this ancient monastery has served as a hostel for travelers for more than a thousand years. Monks and local guides—with the help of their dogs—often had to rescue people who became lost or injured on their way through the mountain pass. Saint Bernard dogs are no longer officially part of the mountain rescue program, but some still live at the hospice. To this day, if you are lucky enough to visit Switzerland, you can stay overnight at the hospice and meet them there.

Barry, the most famous of the Great Saint Bernard rescue dogs, lived from 1800 to 1814. He was involved in many rescues—forty, according to the plaque on his monument in the Cimitière des Chiens (Dog Cemetery) outside Paris. Barry was clearly a very brave dog, but so many legends grew up about him that it is difficult to know exactly which parts are true. One story, for example, is that he was killed when he tried to dig an injured soldier out of the snow. Thinking he was being attacked by a wolf, the soldier stabbed Barry. Fortunately, we know that this is not how Barry really met his death. He retired safely to live in the Swiss city of Bern. In fact, when he died of old age, his body was preserved and displayed in the Bern Museum (where you can still see it today).

I have woven together elements from the

various stories to come up with an imaginary version of what might have happened if, when Barry was still a youngster learning the ropes on a rescue mission, he had bumped into the Time Dogs. Their rescue of Luca from the cave is based on one of the most famous stories about Barry, in which he rescued a child from an ice cavern and carried him on his back to safety. (There is some dispute about whether Barry could really have carried a child, as he was much smaller than the Saint Bernard dogs of today. In the current story, he has lots of help from Maia and the pack, of course!)

The other characters at the Great Saint Bernard Hospice—both human and canine—are all fictional. I invented Brother Francis, Luca, and his mother, as well as Bella, Brio, Bianca, and her puppies. I also invented Kyra the eagle— although golden eagles really do fly over the Swiss Alps.

However, one other character in my story is based on a real dog. Moustache, a large black poodle, was born in 1799. As a young dog he tagged along with an army regiment passing through his hometown of Caen in France. He enjoyed military life so much that he stayed with the French army until he was killed by a cannon-ball in 1812.

There are many stories about Moustache's great exploits: catching a spy, fighting a German dog, rescuing the French flag, being wounded in battle on several occasions. Just as for Barry, the details of Moustache's adventures vary from one account to another. However, we do know that this super-loyal dog accompanied his regiment when Napoleon led the army across the Great Saint Bernard Pass into Italy in the spring of 1800. There is a story that during the crossing, Moustache sniffed out some enemy soldiers who were planning an ambush. He barked a warning and saved his troops.

As far as I know, there is no evidence that Barry and Moustache actually met at the Great Saint Bernard Hospice, but it is at least possible. Barry was a puppy in spring 1800, when Moustache crossed the Alps. This is the story of what might have happened if a meeting between these two famous dogs had taken place—and if the Time Dogs had been there, too! For their adventure together, I combined elements of the story about Barry digging a soldier out of the snow and Moustache warning his troops about an ambush.

You may have noticed that Barry does not introduce himself as a Saint Bernard. This is because the breed name "Saint Bernard" did not come into use until later in the nineteenth century. In Barry's time, the mountain rescue dogs were smaller and lighter than the modern breed and went by various names, including Alpine mastiff. Also, you have probably seen pictures of rescue dogs with little barrels of brandy around their necks. As far as we know, the dogs of the Great Saint Bernard Hospice didn't really wear these; it's an image that became popular after a famous painting by the British artist Edwin Landseer.